MW01286347

I

c

o

p

e

Copyright © 2016 Carolyn Zaikowski
All rights reserved.
CCM Design by *Michael J Seidlinger*
Cover Design by *Ryan W. Bradley*
Interior Design by *Olivia Croom*
ISBN - 978-1-937865-64-1

For more information, find CCM at:

http://copingmechanisms.net

In a Dream, I Dance by Myself, and I Collapse

Carolyn Zaikowski

For Courtney, Catie, and Chris

To forget a friend is sad. Not everyone has had a friend. And if I forget him, I may become like the grown-ups who are no longer interested in anything but figures.

—Antoine de Saint-Exupéry, *The Little Prince*

CONTENTS

I.
ANNOUNCEMENT
PREPARATIONS AND CONSIDERATIONS
1

II.
PRELIMINARY ASSESSMENT
HELPFUL CHECKLISTS
13

III.
ASSESSMENT INTERVIEW
27

IV.
HOW TO BECOME A BETTER SOCIOPATH
HOW TO OVERCOME AN ADDICTION
HOW TO ESTABLISH A FENCE
HOW TO OVERCOME A FEAR
35

IV.
CASE STUDIES #1–5

V.
ANNOUNCEMENT
CHECK-IN
57

VI.
ANNOUNCEMENT
INTERMEDIATE ASSESSMENT
67

VII.
CASE STUDIES #6–12

VIII.
FINAL ASSESSMENT
ANNOUNCEMENT
105

IX.
FINAL ANALYSES

PREFACE

There's a father. There's a father, a mother, a brother. No, no mother. There's a brother, then there's not a brother. Someone tells a lie, crumples it up, sits on it, pulls it out from under them, puts it in the first available mouth. No one knows who did what or who did anything. There's a grandfather and eventually he tries to kill himself, doesn't succeed, and has five operations to fix his eyes. There's a grandfather but soon there won't be one because he'll either just die, or break and die. There's suddenly a mother but she doesn't know she's a mother. The father broke the news, you had my baby, you had my baby. There's a mother who doesn't know anything and a father too, and he'll always be there but we can't see him anymore because of his stupid stupid orphanage heart, the one he will never return from.

Sometimes adults don't believe things because they aren't true.

Sometimes adults don't believe things because they are true.

Sometimes adults don't believe things because they are stupid assholes.

Sometimes nothing happens which means there is a crack that somebody lives in.

There's a lover and a lover's lover. There are all kinds of lovers. There are big ones and small ones, purple ones and brown ones, who all get old and die and everyone's surprised.

I.
ANNOUNCEMENT

PREPARATIONS AND
CONSIDERATIONS

ATTENTION

You live in the universe, which is spectacular. Please drop everything you are doing, go outside, gather your loved ones, and look at something noteworthy. Do not return to your daily life until you have made sure that everything is accounted for.

Thank you.

PREPARATIONS AND CONSIDERATIONS

Congratulations on your decision to embark on a personal journey towards interpersonal and existential effectiveness. The following points may be helpful to keep in mind:

1. At times, downplay your emotion(s) for the sake of getting results. Come to your wise mind.

2. Educate your partner on who you are. Remember that we don't all communicate from the same framework.

3. What if you really got what you were longing for? Would you be able to handle it?

4. Contemplate the difference between *longing for the unrealistic versus longing for something that's actually missing.*

5. The fact that you can't have and know everything is the thing.

6. Practice reframing your cognitive distortions.

7. Observe your attachments to certain states of existence.

8. Sometimes it is not enough to be kind and giving. Sometimes your psyche must be a deep sea diver.

Please keep me updated on your progress and let me know if you need anything. My phone number and address can be found in the secret place behind the bookshelf.

Here is an opposite way to tell the story that actually isn't mine:

First of all, I might not be telling you everything. Secondly, this could be an accident. But I am happy. All is well. Everything around me bursts with life and hope, like an eternal field full of god's tallest and most well-behaved sunflowers. Everything is white, yellow, and orange—in fact, those are the only colors my eyes know how to see. A child swimming deep in my heart-water giggles with excitement on Christmas Eve. She eats too many potato chips, but the excitement counteracts any feeling of oily vomit forming in her stomach. The Christmas tree is majestic and never reminds me of pain.

You are a precious gift; your patterns are remarkable, defiant; you are not bent on definition, you who moves and plays, you who does not try to gain ownership over your various volcanic positions, your lava, your flow to the ocean, your sand. You, my concise mountain, are free. We float through the most intimate kind of universe, fucking everything with our best selves, and you hold me at the blur. You take me right into the explosion of the container. We are

positive that we know the name of the flux. My hands
smell like your spit and skin; fingers are pointed
downwards in an arch. The words are in front of you,
in the air; you use my hands to touch them. I allow
you to take them on a picnic at the top of a mountain.
I want you to be that oddest number, to be its meal.
You are weather. You are entire atmospheres; you
are a complete algebra. I had to be the person who
believed you because there was no one else available.

Dream—you are bleeding; I am happy. You will
never again negate my existence. You'll stop eating
hamburgers. Dream—I don't dare touch your soft
chin. Dream—I own a map that takes me everywhere I ever need to go on every layer. Dream—I
have never thrown my hair over the balcony for you.
Dream—there are no tall students in white coats
taking notes on how I cry. Dream—I don't remember your tie. I don't remember when we roller-skated
over the geraniums. I wasn't even alive in the 1950's!
I don't remember the famous diplomat's wedding or
the crack in the wall where you thought god might
be living. I've never even met anybody famous. I
don't remember the toaster oven exploding. At
least, I don't think I remember that. I know I don't
remember you.

Life doesn't just have the potential to be a lullaby; it
is already one. I sleep and I dream.

Listen, okay, I never do anything that is a secret; I don't even have benign secrets. I am your most open realm. I remember the past as if it's a completely level plane. You are the wall, not the cracks in the wall. You are glue—you never break, you only put together. You aren't in a casket; you are with me, dancing; together we're safe, far beyond pulses. All this being said, I still don't think it's okay that the seventh dimension makes no sense. In fact, it freaks me the fuck out. It makes me want to crawl into a hole and puke on the cutest, smallest bunny rabbit I can find.

Here's a theory: I'm good enough. You love me.

Alright, this time's real, it's the best math I have:

She points to the mirror and tells me to look for the
Buddha's eyes. Instead I look at you. I tell you you're
god's face but you don't believe me. I don't believe
you when you say anything about my face either. I
don't want to reconcile all the different ways in which
I want to love, but the world doesn't like it when
people love without formulas, so maybe it'd be easier
to just forget about you. To go to a place where your
thunderstorm will never make it to my air. Where I
will be so cold that I'll turn to silver. I know you; if
I don't let this go, you will start to engage in one of
your infamous campaigns of self-control. They'll call
your name over the intercom when it is time to die.
"You You YOU." The book I recommended will make
you cry. It'll make you think of the people you've lost,
especially the next time you crane your neck to look
for a plane or branch. I knew all this when I told you
about the book, but I did not want you to be afraid.
I know you—you are not a torn flower or a muti-
lated soldier. You are a bookcase. An upright piano,
perfectly wooden.

"Ale? Cider? Lager? Ale? Cider? Lager?"

Forget it. Tonight, the injured squirrel drags two broken legs behind her like a human who's fallen from a wheelchair. Past a car tire, under a fence, she pulls herself all the way up a tree with the strength of her front paws, her back legs dangling like hair from a head or steaks from meat hooks. She sits in a nook, her breath as still and calm as a Buddha's. I put my hand over my mouth and whisper, What the hell's a Buddha? I call the wildlife rescue hotline but they're closed and I don't have a box to put her in, like they recommend on the automated message, or a car to take her to the shelter when it opens. So I go to the bar and drink beer alone.

"Ale? Cider? Lager? Ale? Cider? Lager?"

"Electricity on the rocks, please."

Give me another chance.

"They've got a different reservation? I don't understand the meaning of this."

"I can't tell you until I see your I.D."

"Look, here is my hand."

"No."

"But look."

"I need to see your I.D."

"Here are my ears."

"There's no place to put you. I'm sorry."

II.
PRELIMINARY ASSESSMENT

HELPFUL CHECKLISTS

PRELIMINARY ASSESSMENT

**Your memory is in your body and in the bodies
of everything that took part in making you. Do
you agree or disagree? Place a check next to the
answers which most represent your desire to be
understood as an existence:**

A) yes   E) blue tyranny

B) no   F) existential mist, or, wrought iron fence

C) yesno   G) omelet or other food

D) I don't get the question

**Do you or do you not own a history within your
finger or other small body part that you may or may
not have an awkward encounter with at some point
in the future:**

A) yes

B) no

C) I do enjoy the frosting on a cake

D) I'm a feminist

Mark the selection which most accurately portrays the outlandish pain of your disappeared lover:

A) Significant soul-dance over clouds of satiety and its opposite

What kind of geometry do you inhabit? Check all that apply:

A) over winding roads

B) past long-winded conversations about god

C) there still will never be

D) another like you

Please place an X above the choices that most resonate with various fur/hairlines across various bodies that you may or may not inhabit:

I am attracted to an invisibility that haunts me on Wednesdays.

Strongly Agree   Agree   No Opinion   Disagree   Strongly Disagree

When you are in comfort, what is the name of your pain?

Strongly Agree   Agree   No Opinion   Disagree   Strongly Disagree

Have you ever encountered a medium-sized desire for travel in and through the Land of the Monstrous Need?

---

definitely   maybe not   never   maybe   definitely, at the
                                                             dawn of a
                                              particularly
                                    painful boundary

or, the difference
between mauve
and brown

Please indicate your personal regard for the life forms unlike you, as you are in your present form:

---

bursting coattails!   ectoplasm side-remark   yes regularly catching   the secret of the

wind of rumor   sphinx turns

my heart-place spectacular

HELPFUL CHECKLISTS

Sleep Hygiene Checklist

__ Is your alarm clock set to the correct time? Are you sure?

__ Are you calm?

__ Are you listening to soothing music and/or reading a light book?

__ Did you refrain from consuming caffeine and alcohol today?

__ Did you remember to take your medications?

__ Did you paint your walls sky blue?

__ Did you have a light, plain snack before you came to bed?

__ Have you purchased a sound machine that mimics the soothing flow of the sea and surrounding lighthouses?

__ Have you lit a safe, scented candle or incense stick?

__ Did you pray?

__ Have you let everybody know how much you love
   them in case you don't wake up?

__ Did you remember to put an inspirational quote
   on the ceiling above your bed so that it is the first
   thing you see when you wake up, provided you
   wake up at all?

__ Did you put away your knives?

__ Did you make sure the oven was off and the
   curling iron unplugged so as to not start an unnecessary fire in the night?

Coping Mechanisms Checklist

__ Shower (scalding)

__ Meditate

__ Drink tea beside lamp

__ Hold your nephew until he falls asleep

__ One moment in this silly and unbelievable universe

__ Hypothesis-theory-law-hypothesis-theory-law

__ Tell what you are afraid of

__ Spy on what you are afraid of

__ Sleep into it

Annihilation Panic Checklist

__ Hair falls out and sticks to sides of shower

__ Nails are blue and crunchy

__ You shit yourself in public

__ There is a twitch

__ Bones break

__ Infertility becomes you

__ Various nodes swell

__ You wear three blankets and four sweatshirts on
    hottest day of summer

__ There is hair growth, especially on cheek

__ There is obsession

__ There is pride

__ An organ ruptures

__ Sensory over-stimulation occurs

__There is longing

__ Synesthesia happens

__ Maybe there's a cliff

Irrational Beliefs Checklist

__ The wine that is eternity's blood should not be imbibed

__ I must fix broken things

__ It is possible for something to be broken

__ I must not tell a lie

__ Heart-things can and should be defined

__ I should do everything my neurosis tells me to

__ I should apologize for existing

__ Life should be saved even when it doesn't want to be

__ I should look away from the darkest part

__ I must never tell you what I see

__ I must never unconditionally love a stranger

__ Intensity should be stored in a compact container

__ I should change the pace of my soul's metabolism

__ Hunger does not need a name

__ Ghosts don't exist

__ Your story should not be told

__ You are going to be gone now, too

III.
ASSESSMENT INTERVIEW

ASSESSMENT INTERVIEW

INTERVIEWER: Please speak carefully into this microphone. It is the most sensitive microphone that exists. My first question is, tell me about your mother's memories, which you may or may not hold inside of your own body- muscles, aorta, etc.

SUBJECT: The memory of my mother's first pencil. Or when she was seven and her parents sent her to the neighbor's house at night so they could go to wherever it is you go to identify the dead body of a loved one. I remember the shape of the room where she painted nudes in art school, and what the bus smelled like upon which she met my dad… I think it smelled like diesel mixed with some baked goods that resonated in her nose from that morning. I think, perhaps, her roommate had baked apple pie. I remember where she was standing when and if my father threw a beer can at her, hit her in the room with all the couches watching.

A face. A squished face my mother wanted to make at the person selling coffee and banana bread in the cafeteria at the office building, in 1979. She never ended up making the face because she felt shame for the compulsion even though everyone around her wished that somebody would open the door to that type of clownery just once in that place where nothing seemed to live. A path to the city of her dreams made of time and tubes; this I know for sure.

The color of her right hand clenching god as she birthed my older brother. I sat on top of the windowsill watching and this was before disco—no, wait—I mean, they would have been playing disco in that room if it existed, right?

INTERVIEWER: Right. Tell me about your own entirety.

SUBJECT: In London, my grandmother watched bombs scatter from far away. She sold pounds and pounds of sugar and gallons and gallons of milk to the city folk. Back then, everybody saved their buttons and string. She touches my cheek and her soft skin is a tarp of time, and she remembers her husband is dying in her wrinkles and bunions. She never speaks of him but wants to. I remember how my mother's ankles and feet flew, her heart cracked out a symphony and she ran out of the room because her father was dead on the bottom stair. His head was under a painting. Was it one of her own paintings? I do not remember whether or not she went to the neighbor's house this time.

I remember when my mother was... eight? Nine? Ten? And the lake house in Maine hadn't been hit by the legendary hurricane yet. Nobody knew yet. I waited for myself and it to arrive. It's weird for a hurricane to get all the way to Maine. The trees are still there. Well, a couple of them. Actually, no.

Mostly that forest is populated by jet skis and rich people now. That forest in Maine where the hurricane made it at last.

And I remember the color of my mother's shoes when she married my father in the backyard of my grandmother's house but I cannot tell you about that color the only hint I will give you is that it is not the same color as the shoes she wore to court to sign divorce papers on Valentine's Day a few years later. When she got married in the yard I'm pretty sure she looked at the black ring around the oak tree and recalled the summer of the gypsy moths. My mother, she doesn't know whether or not she remembers certain things. But I will keep it all for her if she doesn't want to hold it. I'll keep it in case she wants to... paint. Destroy. Remember. Deny. Change it, think it. In case she wants to pummel it all with rocks and flaming arrows. Like I want to whenever I think about the universe and its various hands hurting her.

INTERVIEWER: Is that all of everything?

SUBJECT: It's not even a little bit. Look, my grandmother's hair was brown when my mom was born. It was even brown when I was born. And she was always tall. My grandmother says she used to be 5'7". Then she was 5'4". Since all of the operations, she's 5'1". My grandmother's back is slowly breaking; four of her vertebrae have slipped apart like pants being unzipped. The only thing that's in my control now is my own ability to sit next to her. That's the only thing that's ever been in my control which is terrible in a really wonderful way.

My grandmother likes her white hair. When two months ago I asked her, "What's one thing you like about yourself?" that's what she said—"My white hair. I feel so liberated now that I've stopped dyeing it!"

INTERVIEWER: And what of your own body's relationship to change?

SUBJECT: I was small, silent, and female and my greatest achievement was my long blonde hair. At thirteen I cut it off and died it blue. My family still asks me when I'm going to grow my hair back. I tell them, when they read my novel. I don't really tell them that.

INTERVIEWER: What does your body say?

I don't know what my body says. I don't listen to it. I don't know where my body would go if it could ask. My teeth want to tell a story but I disregard them. One of my teeth has a hole in it and if you look real close you can see the inside. Generally I tend to swivel into the position which finds me. My body's voices are indistinguishable from laughter, pain, and numbness. I would like for somebody to give me a bar to hold that is attached to something other than my own body, so that I don't ever have to float alone again. Actually, it could be that none of what I just said is true.

INTERVIEWER: So, then, challenge god.

SUBJECT: Okay. I challenge god to a game of Parcheesi with my grandmother. Him against us. No, wait, I challenge god to a write-off. I challenge god to a duel which involves the fate of man's relationship with himself. By which I mean, to men's relationships with themselves. I challenge god to drink whiskey with me. Does god drink whiskey? Hm. I've never thought about that before. If not, then what's his drink of choice? I'm willing to bet it's water. I bet god doesn't drink bottled water because I bet god knows plastic water bottles are a waste and that recycling, while good in some respects, is really just a liberal environmentalist band-aid on what's pretty much like an arm that's falling off a body, dangling by a string of flesh, and you can't fix that with a band-aid unless you have a big-ass band-aid—

INTERVIEWER: We've got to move on. Please speak to me about air.

SUBJECT: Listen. From a cough you get eternity. From a cough—right into eternity. From a cough into space. From a cough into syntax. From a cough I blow a butterfly towards an orange.

INTERVIEWER: Reply to your breath—relate to it as simply as you can.

SUBJECT: I can't do that.

INTERVIEWER: Why?

SUBJECT: I'm scared.

INTERVIEWER: Fill your space with words.

SUBJECT: No.

INTERVIEWER: Let me put this differently: Transmit your experience through sound.

SUBJECT: Fine. Oooooggghhh, crshhhhhh crshhhh, gahhhhhh, wonkwonkwonkwonk, wonk.

INTERVIEWER: Are you ready to experience whatever happens?

SUBJECT: I'm not sure. But I don't have much of a choice if whatever is going to happen happens anyway so my answer has to be yes.

INTERVIEWER: Tell me a story.

SUBJECT: In New Hampshire, I saw lichens on a rock. This is a true story that happened.

IV.

HOW TO BECOME
A BETTER SOCIOPATH

HOW TO OVERCOME
AN ADDICTION

HOW TO ESTABLISH A FENCE

HOW TO OVERCOME A FEAR

HOW TO BECOME A BETTER SOCIOPATH

RING

You are a *sociopath*. Basically what this means, is that you have an inability to relate to the pain of others. Your emotional system is a different make and model than the norm and, most likely, you have never felt the thing that most people think of as empathy. Many people in civilized society consider this problematic to some degree. Terms often used interchangeably with *sociopath* include

psychopath and *antisocial personality*.

In this section you will learn to associate images of muddy footprints with your sociopathic tendencies. We will begin by invoking some of your sense memories of maiming people, which will include the process of having you describe, both out loud and on paper, your maiming memories, as we slowly surround you with pictures of weapons and corpses. We will measure your heart rate and other vital signs to make sure you reach your maximum. When your body reaches this heightened state of arousal in relation to maiming, the bell will ring to indicate the desired association, at which point we will clamp your eyelids open and you will view a panoramic image of a generic muddy footprint.

RING

Now you are to listen to the bell five more times, and each time it rings you will see the image of the generic muddy footprint. As this happens, you should begin to notice an increasing drive to violently confront the footprint. We will do this several times today and you will return for six more weeks of treatment.

RING RING RING RING RING

When we have finished with this series of treatments, your propensity towards violence and its new relationship with muddy footprints should successfully be triggered by the sound of a bell, anywhere, at any time.

HOW TO OVERCOME AN ADDICTION

Detox (detoxification): Many professionals believe that the first step in overcoming the addictive process is to engage in *detoxification*. This may be done in several different ways. You may have a trusted loved one come to your house and lock you in your bedroom for a predetermined amount of time. Have your trusted loved one open the door only to bring you food as needed.

Often, people who are undergoing *detoxification* find ways to access their addictive behavior, even if they are locked in a room. For instance, if you are a self-mutilator, you may tape a knife to a very secret place behind the toilet bowl, or you may figure out a way to hurt yourself with something as simple as a pencil or fingernail. You know this, but the trusted loved one may not be so aware of the subtleties of addiction. Therefore, if you must leave your bedroom to go to the bathroom, you must let your trusted loved one accompany you. They should even watch you go to the bathroom to make sure that you are not engaging in any addictive behaviors. This might be embarrassing, but if all goes well, you will thank them later. They might be saving your life.

Alternatively, you may bring yourself, or have someone else bring you, to a hospital where the doctors will be the ones to lock you in a room and proceed as they see fit.

For more information on overcoming an addiction, see *How to Overcome a Fear.*

HOW TO ESTABLISH A FENCE

Establishing a fence is a highly personal and practical process. There are several routes you can take to establish your fence.

First, you will need to ask yourself, what is the purpose of this fence? What location will maximize this purpose? When you have figured these things out, you will want to create a realistic timetable for the construction of your fence. Keep in mind that fences generally cannot be built in a day. In fact, sometimes it takes several failures before you build the most effective fence. Remember that failure is part of the fence-building process.

Next you will want to make a list of the materials needed to build your fence. Some people find that their fence needs to be made of wood or metal; other people prefer to make fences out of their soul-parts, or their skin. Refer back to your fence's main purpose to deduce what materials you will need.

Many people find it effective to establish a fence around their arms or hands. Others find that they need a fence around their house or their heart.

When you have completed your fence, you will need to authorize it. You can do this by embracing the fence as fully as possible and saying, "I have established you. Now I cannot be touched."

HOW TO OVERCOME A FEAR

Behavioral Therapy: If you are afraid of a snake, you can become gradually or instantly habituated to it by placing yourself in the vicinity of the snake. This method is called *exposure*. You may hire a behavioral therapist to help you in this process, but—and this is a secret because they want you to pay for it—you can also do it by yourself. This process might take place over time; for instance, you might visit the forest where the snake lives. The next day, perhaps you will stand within twenty feet of the snake, and the day after that, ten feet. One day, you will approach the snake and stand right next to her. After that, when you are ready in your heart, you might touch the snake or even hold her. At this point the snake may tell you the biggest secret in all the world. You might never have known that secret had you never trusted her.

Cognitive Behavioral Therapy (CBT): With the help of a professional who has an ostensibly objective lens with which to view your torturous neuroses, you can learn to decipher the triangular dance between the attitudes, behaviors, and emotions that occurs in response to your fears. For instance, if you have anorexia and you are experiencing the EMOTION of ANXIETY around becoming a normal sized person, your cognitive behavioral therapist may ask you, "What is the THOUGHT behind FEAR (YOUR EMOTION)?" And you may reply, "My thought is that if I eat this I will explode and die." And your cognitive behavioral therapist will then point out to you that you are having an irrational thought. This may make you feel even more insane. However, many have reported that, after several sessions, cognitive behavioral therapy works the miracles of god.

Psychotherapy (Talk therapy; counseling): Recommended only under conditions of extreme and enduring mental and psycholinguistic flux.

V.
CASE STUDIES #1–5

#1: Courtney
#2: May 6th
#3: Catie
#4: Asheville
#5: Everyone Dies in Boston

CASE STUDY #1: Courtney

"I can't wait to ask god where he got those sweet shorts."

For years, I have been used to the way her head only reaches my shoulder. Maybe it doesn't even reach that high; she is approximately eight inches shorter than me. She is always asking me to grab cups and plates, candles and cake, from the top shelf because she can't reach them.

She cuts the sleeves off her shirts when it is humid, never thinking about what she will do for shirts come winter. She is the personification of the color blue. Her eyes, hair, teeth, and skin are blue. She sleeps with only a thin screen separating her from a family of blue raccoons who try, every night, to destroy her air conditioner. Her goldfish floats upside down due to a digestive problem and her cat has twenty-four toes. She forever mourns the death of her hermit crab; she did not mean to fall in love with him. She dreams of wearing leggings, of moving to Seattle, of saving things.

Her spurts of creativity come at the most inopportune times. In the middle of the night, she calls out to the world for adventures, wants to read poems to the universe, paint pictures onto an eternity she can't find; at three in the morning she wants to bulldoze the Cape Cod cranberry bogs, jump in front of the bulldozer, make soup out of all of the roots and vines and dirt she recovers from it.

It's a humid July afternoon when we ask god to have iced tea with us. We boil the water and put it in a big pot because we can't find a proper pitcher. We fill the pot up with Lipton's tea bags and watch the sienna clouds melt into the hot water. We put the tea in the refrigerator, let it cool for about an hour, fill it up with ice cubes and a few lemon slices. We leave the sugar out; we figure we should let god decide whether or not he wants his iced tea sweetened. We decorate the table with dead flowers in empty wine bottles.

We are in a stadium, which is actually the universe. It's god's birthday. He is sixty-five trillion years old.

"I wonder what day it was when he created the pencil sharpener? Pavement?"

The owl tattooed on her shoulder winks at me as we talk about sex, about collaborative art, about other people's relationships. On her hip, which she doesn't always know is a wonderful one, three tattooed stars remind us of dead friends.

I was with her the day the Mooninites took over Boston. 1/31/07: Never forget.

As we wait for god, we roll joints, wondering whether or not we should give one to him as a birthday present, but decide against it. We sew punk rock patches on our skirts. We ask the universe-waiter for band-aids. We take pictures of ourselves showing our teeth, then hiding our teeth. God was supposed to be here at five-thirty. It's almost nine.

"I don't think he's coming. He's probably super busy today."

We are a finished puzzle. We swallow our Prozac with coffee and red wine. We are only sometimes ashamed.

CASE STUDY #2: May 6th

What it really is, is that my dog is dying. And he's
my last link to you, who did that thing too. The
universe felt so hugely stupid the day you died. It
was a Sunday. It was May sixth. It was three years
ago. I sat on the muddy porch like a shaved peacock,
undone. What's a somebody without a body? Right.
At night it's like I can feel you, and when I wake up
you've died again, even though it means nothing to
keep dying. But I cannot help my skin; it has gone so
far past me, you wouldn't believe how far. You're like
lead. You're all me now. Just me.

I look to my little friend and hold both our breaths,
thinking maybe I can keep him a little longer, thinking maybe I need him to help me grow my feathers
back. But maybe he just wants to be with you since
you went and did the stupid thing like he's about
to. Maybe there was a certain way you scratched his
left ear or tapped his stomach that I never mastered;
unlike me, you were always quite nuanced. I know
this seems irrational, but sometimes I think he sees
you, filters you through some sensory pocket I'll
never access. When he drinks water from the secret
swimming place and has those spasms of his tongue,
I'm like, "You. You." Then I convince myself life's
an infection, and you were cured by running just fast
enough. Then I think, this might be the definition of
loneliness, of being an earth invader.

CASE STUDY #3: Catie

"I want to make things with other things. I want to
make rocks into spaceships with hammers for wings."

She is taking careful notes on how to melt record
albums in the oven. She read somewhere that if you do
it at the perfect temperature, for just the right amount of
time, you can get them to a malleable consistency. She
wants to turn them into bowls and sell them in the park.

"Okay? We have to go clean off some records. After
that we make a chandelier out of recycled jars."

She wants me to use my hands. She tries to teach
me how to engage with physical materials. Her mind
works through her skin.

"You can make coffee tables out of anything. Not just
flat things. I'm talking, like, old computers. Dried up
teabags. Batteries. Guitars."

There are so many things hanging on her walls: broken
skateboard decks, a plastic gorilla bank, guitars, fris-
bees; in the corner near the top of the closet, there is a
paint brush stuck to the wall, thick with neon pink.

A drawing of a girl with no face. A Buddha, backwards. Self-portraits in charcoal. A flimsy tapestry
that I bought for her in Bihar.

She drinks Kombucha. She writes country songs even though she is from a city in the North. She takes photographs of invisible things. She can't believe I haven't seen *E.T.* She loves avocado. She has one dreadlock.

We have the same initials; we carve them into the wooden pole at the rest stop in the mountains. We spend weeks perfecting our recipe for vegan fudge. We cry when we say goodbye to the harmless dog. We stare at the redwoods. We give granola bars, juice, and mixed nuts to the homeless man. We swim naked in the lake and hide underwater when hikers pass. We write songs that we don't tell anyone about. We get stoned and make the ugliest faces possible. At the cleanest river we've ever seen, we find god rippling. We take pictures of our bruises. We spray paint sidewalks at night. We drink whole bottles of red wine while watching game shows. We show each other our bodies and, for the first time in our lives, we aren't scared. This is a secret.

She looks at me as I stand in the mirror. She tells me to make my own world. To crash and burn. She teaches me to never be afraid of rust.

CASE STUDY #4: Asheville

In Asheville, I am drinking a beer in the back of a record store. A friend cries as he plays the guitar.

We meet a woman we call Georgia Peach. She is sixty years old and has been coloring her own hair since she was sixteen. She doesn't want to think about how many years have gone by. "I'd dance if my foot wasn't so bad off," she announces to the banjo player on the sidewalk.

Yesterday in Virginia, the Astrovan broke down. On Interstate 81 a country band in a biodiesel bus picked us up and brought us here. After rescuing vegetable oil and bagels from a dumpster, we drove the bus up a mountain and almost tipped over into a creek. I stayed up all night in the house on the mountain, talking to you about Buddhism, nonviolence theory, monogamy, sweat, and creeks.

I'm in charge of watching Georgia Peach's belongings while she limps up the street to buy Eddie Bauer jeans for a dollar and refill her prescriptions.

On the side of the road, under a bridge, I cry because I have no money. I imagine the following things

–What it would be like to walk in front of a car

–Calling you even though you won't answer

–The profile of your ghost in front of me

and then I scold myself. I want to see you from this angle. I want you to be vulnerable.

Let it go... let it go. Fly. On Route 81, the lights turn on by themselves. I think that'll make you happy, if you're ever here. Let's drive over small bridges and dizzy mountains. Let's listen to Johnny Cash and The Boss. Let's try to get through Dutch Country tonight. I have a tent if you have a field.

CASE STUDY #5: Everyone Dies in Boston

Boston is a city in Massachusetts, which is a state on the eastern coast of the United States of America. Boston is hot. You may not know this. You may think that Boston is cold and blustery, which is also true. But sometimes, it is so hot that people want to die, so they do. This summer, everyone in Boston has decided to die.

I've reached this conclusion based on several pieces of evidence. One is that everybody had a meeting at the park on Sunday and said, "We are going to die this summer." The next piece of evidence is that Millie drove her car into a guardrail, punctured her lung, and fractured her skull. Then Molly hung herself from a bridge downtown. Then Maggie was murdered by the person who said he loved her. Then May tried to starve herself to death, which didn't work, so she joined the military.

All over Boston, there are bikes painted white and flowers taped to telephone poles, jars for collecting memorial donations, murals of faces that don't exist. The famous homeless man can't pay for his funeral. The girl I love gets hit by a car and her body is too small to retain blood. The girl I love falls asleep and never wakes up. The boy I love drives his car into a field and never returns. The body is hanging from the bridge with grace.

January 15, 1919 was the date of the Boston
Molasses Disaster, which is sometimes called the
Great Molasses Flood or the Great Boston Molasses
Tragedy. A huge molasses tank, holding 2.3 million
gallons of the substance, exploded in the North End,
creating a sticky tsunami that poured through the
town at about forty miles per hour and at a pressure
of two tons per square foot. Hundreds of humans,
horses, dogs, cats, vehicles, and houses were tossed
into the air; others were sucked under and crushed;
still others were helplessly stuck to the rolling wave
as the neighbors watched in horror. A train was lifted
off the elevated tracks and thrown. Sewers were
clogged. The molasses flooded the Boston Harbor,
which ran brown all the way through the summer.
It is said that the whole city smelled of sugar for
months. After hundreds of workers sifted through
the destruction, it was declared that twenty-one
humans were killed by the molasses tsunami, and 150
injured. Local legend has it that, on humid summer
days, the winding North End streets still smell faintly
sweet. Although the explosion was likely caused by
the faulty and haphazard design of the molasses tank,
authorities were quick to blame the Anarchists.

So the plane crashed, the bridge collapsed, and in
Boston it will smell like embers and molten molasses
for two hundred more years. This is how I know the
war will never end.

VI.
ANNOUNCEMENT

CHECK-IN

ATTENTION

The bars on the jail have decided to revolt. Please drop everything you are doing, gather your loved ones, and quietly assist the bars in detaching themselves from the ceiling and floor. Do not return to your daily life until they are all free and safe.

Thank you.

CHECK-IN

Dear lady: I saw you, singing, in the grass between
two trees. In the background a mountain was ironing
a sky, which was a universe-movement I grew fond
of and found myself thinking about several hours
later. It seemed you and your friends were pretending
to be clowns. The art of the clown just isn't taken
seriously in this country. Do me a favor. Photocopy
your aura for me. Make sure you use the color copier.
Photocopy your mind for me, like how we used to
photocopy our middle fingers when we were little, in
the library, how we'd giggle. Send the copies to me,
I will write poems on them and send them back to
you and then you can make another photocopy on
top of that. In your soul, there is a snare drum that
stutters. It haunts me; I cry for you. And sometimes
I cry because my favorite dress doesn't fit anymore
because of all the weight I've gained since becoming
reasonable. I have been hoarding my breath, I get
scared of air. I forget that the world holds me, always.
Love you

Dear lady: So I said to him, you are not Buddha. You
are not Jack Kerouac. You are not even John Lennon.
You are a generic man who's continually intruding on
my psychological space. You make me feel like I am
being jerked off on. The whole time you're going off,
I'm just thinking to myself, make some fucking room.
Anyways, I hope you enjoy this zine I'm sending. It's

about peak oil. Peak oil is becoming a serious issue you know. Be home soon, maybe—Love you P.S. Dream—I can't find my luggage; I can't find you.

My illusive lady: I make love only to notebooks. You are reading the results of those unions. Unorthodox, I know. Don't judge me. I'm sure there are plenty of things you do that could be construed as shameful. You should feel special that I am letting you be such a voyeur...special like a tall, tall sunflower in a beautiful garden filled with berries and happy rabbits. You do or don't exist. Oh, how I would have worn you either way. Love you

Dearest friend: Can you proofread this for me? Dear B.F. Skinner: What is your feeling on the Theory of Mind as applied to autism? It seems to me that, if framed a certain way, it could be used to view autistic people as sociopaths. Mr. Skinner, I also wanted to ask you: How do you feel about Applied Behavior Analysis? Do you feel it helps or hinders autistic people? I can't be sure and I'm certainly no expert. But it seems that, if used certain ways, under certain circumstances, it might make them into duller versions of themselves. Especially when electric shocks are used. The last thing I want to say, Mr. Skinner, is fuck you and your Skinner Box and your mutilation of rats and pigeons and fuck the fascist experiments you wanted to perform on society as elucidated in your creepy manifesto *Walden Two*.

Fuck the fact that people continue to swing from your fascist balls as is evidenced by the common practice of shocking autistic children and other "weirdos" which I can't help but think you may have approved of, although I'm not sure if you actually had direct involvement with the practice or if people just did it based on your ideas. Oh yeah, and fuck you for evoking the language of Thoreau when you titled your book. Love you

Oh my dear girl: I think about you every time I walk by the black ring around the oak tree. If you buy me a couple beers I will love you and compliment you and touch your hand softly as though I don't know how soft I'm being. I will charm you, sing for you, cradle your head... did you know that love and greed turn into one another under situations of extreme power differential? Greed is a strategy. Sometimes it really works. Self-sufficiency becomes dependent upon needing to take as much as possible in order to feel a sense of control. Holding others so they begin to need you. Taking what is theirs until they become convinced you have what they need which, of course, you do. If others need you, you exist. I will continue this letter later. Love you. P.S. Do you have god's phone number? Can I get it from you? I need to ask that guy a question.

Dear lady: What do you think of the Coriolis Effect? How on different sides of the equator, water turns different ways down the drain? What do you think happens at the exact place where it switches? Do you think the water just goes straight down? What do you think of the hypoglycemic index? How about body mass index? Index cards? The word "collateral"? Since I left, since I pretended to see you, I've found that taking care of someone means many things: catering to, helping, accepting all faults, being the body that can relieve a tortured fist. Taking over another's soul is the essence of domination, you know. Co-opting someone. Erasing their identity as a being. Don't tell anybody, but I know someone who knows how to murder bodies, among other things. I heard someone say "murder is to body what rape is to soul." What do you think? Love you.

My friend: This may be the last time you hear from me for a while. So how bout this—put your pain into mine. We can team up. You feel one day and I'll feel the next. This way we can take breaks and naps. Cooperative pain is useful in this sense. Pain solidarity. Mutual aid. Yeah, you were always such a little radical. "Balancing the rocks on top of one another/ She finds that she is no verb." Love you.

RING

"Hi, is this Joe? Hi Joe. It's Orion—you know, the constellation? I just wanted to let you know that I connected with the mistress. Yeah. I'm checking it

out. I'm up here for a week. Thinking about driving
south a little. I'll see what I can set up. Thanks so
much for being a superlative example of life. Bye."

RING

"Hi, is this Chris? Yeah, this is Orion the constellation—how'd you know? Hah! Yeah, got lost last
night but ended up finding a temple to stay at, over
near the golf course in the canyon. Would love to
ascertain your personal description of the universe at
some point. Thanks man. Talk to you Friday."

VII.
ANNOUNCEMENT

INTERMEDIATE ASSESSMENT

ATTENTION

Those you deem speechless are trying to tell you the secrets of pain. Please gather all of your loved ones, go to those you deem speechless and decode their movements and noises. Realize they do indeed speak, but you do not open your ears wide enough. Please do not return to your daily life until you have been more creative in regards to your conception of what mouths, ears, and pain can be.

Thank you.

INTERMEDIATE ASSESSMENT

In a kind and timely manner, please consider the below questions and send them to me through the pipe we talked about.

1. The truth swivels and swings like a song. Clouds can swivel and so can countries. Make a list that represents the swiveling of your past.

2. What is your rock? What is the gender and race of your rock? Has your rock experienced pleasure, privilege, and/or oppression? Is your rock one million and sixty-four years old and does it understand, on the deepest level available, both the molecular formation of iron and the extinction of species? Worm holes in the space-time continuum could very well exist. Does your rock know that? Does it know that the universe might be like a half-deflated balloon folding over itself, the ends touching each other, and that if this is true, then it might be able to leap through this time/space to another time/space? Is your rock wondering: Why aren't brains exploding over this fact? Over the fact that there could be eleven dimensions, and we can see light from the past because time equals space, so therefore, it is reasonable to ask: Can the past and future see us? Is an intelligent alien with

a huge telescope in another galaxy watching dinosaurs walk around? Is it true that, the more your rock thinks about science, the bigger and safer death and life seem? If so, does your rock consider this to be god? To your rock, are exclamation points just a guise for comets? Are galaxies, planets, and quasars eternity's commas and semicolons and ampersands? Does your rock want to rush through the life/sentence?

3. In two complete sentences, please indicate the level of your exposure to instances that are green. Here are some examples:

One time I knew a woman with a voice that was salted and peppered. She never said anything with the letter "E" in it.

A horse spun a web of apples and a spider spun one of leaves. They wanted to bear witness, so they did.

It was not considered elegant to be dying or afraid. It was considered elegant to be large and wonderful with life.

The woman said, "I am decidedly non-animal." She wanted to bear witness, so she did.

The woman wanted to eliminate problematic
behavior; or did she want to make it extinct?
Either way, she held it like a cat or bomb, listening carefully for the initial growl.

You understood what I said. You thanked me
for telling you so much after only knowing you
for ten minutes.

You were scared of being presumptuous. You
had no books with you when you arrived on the
island, alone.

She had the look in her eyes of a mother who
lost a child. But still she smiled.

Thank you for the sepia photographs that you
found in somebody else's trash. I will use them
to write my autobiography.

You had no books with you when you arrived
on the deserted island. Were you so bored that
you drank the salt water?

What you don't know is that I've known you for
way longer than ten minutes. What you don't
know is that I've known you for way longer
than ten minutes.

What washed up with you when you were born?
I'm pretty sure there was a disgruntled sigh in
heaven's womb when I emerged.

Did they want to let me go? Were they happy?

Do you miss your son? Are you happy?

Did the salt water on the island make you
crazy? I had a dream you were falling in love
with an inanimate object.

The woman took her sweet time to disappear.
She wanted to bear witness, so she did.

4. **Please indicate six adjectives that best
   describe your ability to engage in the relationship between dissociation and hyperarousal,
   also known as the remnants of the shattered
   soul. Some examples are** *cautious, caustic,
   relevant, blustery, animal,* **and** *red.*

5. **A lobotomy is a form of psychosurgery in
   which all or some of the prefrontal cortex is
   removed from a human's brain. The prefrontal
   cortex is where the following things happen
   and live: personality traits, planning abilities,
   math, abstract thinking, morals. Lobotomies
   can be performed with both drills and ice
   picks, though historically, the lobotomy**

patient does not get to choose which method
will be used. In this box, please write a state-
ment exploring your thoughts and opinions on
the prefrontal cortex and lobotomies:

6. Addiction can be defined as the compulsion to engage in a certain activity. Addiction is *maladaptive* in that it interferes with an individual's normal, everyday functioning. There is controversy as to whether addictions should be classified as *diseases* or *massive habits*. Examples of addiction include: Drug use, yelling at people, self-mutilation, abusive relationship dynamics, eating, not eating, fast driving, pornography, gambling, internet use, cleaning, turning the light switch on and off, hating oneself, hurting others, breaking things, talking, buying things, stealing, cigarette smoking, working, trying, and leaving. List your addictions in the box provided below. Be creative and honest.

6A. Tell me what you are afraid of. No? Okay, I will:

Everyone misses someone, but I'm afraid of
sleeping you off. Of never remembering you. Of
your face fading in that memory I have of a very
particular tree under which we sat and talked
about the psychology of attraction. I'm afraid of
getting you off. I'm afraid of not getting you off.
I'm afraid of what the piano wanted to say but
couldn't. I was at a yard sale on top of a mountain and I found the book you recommended
to me. It only cost two dollars. When I look at
it now, I think about how you are so filled with
love that it scares me; this makes me so sorry for
not calling. The clock ticks. I'm not just saying
this to be dramatic. The clock is ticking, and it's
one of the only things you can hear, isn't it? I'm
afraid that maybe you can hear some kind of
fan or air vent, too. What if you forget about the
clock? What then? The thing is, you never walk
on this side of the road. This is the one day you
want to be out of the shadow. The movers are
clumsy and drunk. They're pulling the piano up
to the fourth story with thick wires. They drop
the piano on your head. Toccata and Fugue in
D Minor is plunked in its entirety in that one
second it takes you to die.

**7. Please explain your shame in a five-paragraph
essay with introduction, conclusion, and three**

paragraphs that reveal a minimum of three points that you will have referred to in your introduction and will recap in your conclusion. Please use the back of your paper if you need more room but do not exceed the space it takes for a sunflower to grow to maximum height. This is for your use, not mine.

There's some scrunched-up skin. Frenetic wire veins are in and on my body, ruining through and into. Names of streets along the sixty-six bus happen: Parker Hill, Centre Lane, Roxy Crossing, Harvey Warren. At the last stop I go to the lemonade stand which sells brains on the black market, only three hundred calories each, and the vendor tells me I gotta connect. "You're not here!" he says.

Sucking on a quarter of a lemon, I tell him, "You just don't get it. Dreaming is an anti-party: Refrigerated cat carcasses, the challenge of a kill; one solitary bone exists on the eternal cruise ship of human traffic. Across the sea, they send us to the complacent doctor's office where we cannot hide from the vengeance of the chain because the co-pay is two thousand dollars. 'Sorry,' drools the administrative assistant, cupping the rejected credit card. Then the crescendo begins. The mother won't answer the telephone even though the child careens through everything she's sure she hears on the other line. No one seems to be able to properly hold the third falling filling of life pie. Everyone is already too tortured by torte and tangerine flan. This necessitates a bona fide fiery connection to the outbound boat." Understanding nothing about the in-between, spitting out a sour seed, I loudly offer, "Where are *you?*"

8. **How will you be, then?**

I will be with you.

VIII.
CASE STUDIES #6–12

CASE STUDY #6: Sigmund Freud

I'm in a coffee shop in Boston, waiting for Sigmund Freud. I hear someone talking about me: "She's over there. She's tall, she has blonde hair and a Little Prince tattoo." I turn around. The pretty lady with the shawl and the curly brown hair is pointing at my feet. "You dropped a dollar," she mouths. I look down; there's money on the floor. Sigmund is late.

The pretty lady with the shawl comes over to me. "Even though it's already the end of July, I want to ask you: How are you going to spend your summer?"

"Oh, um. I think I'm going to be doing thesis research this summer. I'm going to try researching at different times of the day and under different types of trees in New England. I'm going to use inferential statistics to see how those results compare to the results from the research I did at night in Calcutta, which is actually now called Kolkata, during the monsoon season, when I stood on the balcony alone. Additionally, I've been working on a fourteen-by-ninety factorial design that will, if all goes well, confirm the null hypothesis regarding the efficacy of a meta-analysis of the scientific method."

She turns to the person at the table across from mine, who has a very thick moustache. "How are *you* going to spend your summer?"

"Um, I'm thinking about facial hair this summer." He strokes his moustache. "Great question by the way. This summer, I'm going to see if I can disguise myself as a gardener while plotting the revolution from an inside place."

The pretty lady with the shawl replies, "What do you mean?"

"Look, I'm just trying to stay busy is all," he replies with a coy smile. "I'm doing an experiment on pseudo-liberal self-awareness. I'm planning on some initial skepticism but I think I'll start buying into it eventually, along with everyone else."

"I don't understand..."

"What I'm trying to say is that schools are like warehouses. Can learning really happen in a warehouse? Maybe, if you are exceptionally creative."

The pretty lady with the shawl gets a new look in her eyes. "I don't get you, so I'm going to change the subject. Do you know Sabrina?"

"Yeah, she's my best friend forever!" exclaims the man with the moustache.

"She's my campus manager!" exclaims the pretty lady with the shawl.

"Too cool! Small world! Wow!"

"So maybe we are connected in the cosmos somehow?"

"No."

"We aren't connected in the cosmos?"

"Right."

"I get it because I'm smart."

"I can tell you must have gone to college." The man with the moustache takes a sip from his latte, which happens to be the largest latte I have ever seen. Overcome with the desire to be anonymous, to be the one who haunts him, to be the cat at his windowsill, I move to another table.

Finally Sigmund shows up. He's smoking a pipe and not really paying attention to where he's blowing the smoke. I notice the smoke's heading in a diagonal line, directly towards the moustache on the man at the other table. Sigmund doesn't recognize me, because we've never met. I pretend I don't know who he is; I don't want him to get on an ego trip. He sits down next to me and I ask if I can have his notes. Without hesitation, he gives two notebooks to me— quite a surprise. I didn't think he actually would. "It's all I have," he says. "But if you give me your address, I can FedEx the rest of them to you over night."

"That would be totally awesome," I tell him, writing my address on a napkin.

"So, who are you?" Sigmund asks.

"I don't really want to talk about myself. Can I tell you about this guy I know?"

"Sure."

"Okay... let's see. There's this guy who does repairs on my house, and he's always drunk. One time I saw him drinking tequila on the roof in the middle of the day. When our porch fell in, he fixed it with electrical tape, then painted the electrical tape white so you couldn't really notice it from the street."

"That's nuts!" Sigmund almost chokes on his coffee.

"Are you okay, man?" I ask.

"I'm fine, I'm fine," he replies. "Oh, would you like some of these? They're really good. They're fried mushrooms."

"Oh, no thank you, I'm vegan."

"But they're just mushrooms," he insists.

"They have cheese on them."

"But they're just cheese and mushrooms."

"Look, I'm not really hungry, but thanks. Anyways, one time, I went down into the unfinished part of the basement to find something, behind where we keep all our guitars and drums, and he was back there smoking weed with a friend. He asked me if I was angry... I said, no, just smoke me up and I won't tell the landlord. Then we got wicked stoned."

"Gotta be careful how much of that stuff you smoke! It can make you really wacky," replies Sigmund.

"I know. Down in my basement, there's a hidden door that has a wooden plank over it, and somebody spray painted the words This Is Not An Exit on the door. I think it was him. Have you ever read *American Psycho?*"

"Can't say I have."

"Nevermind. Anyways, this other time, he left a wooden plank in the driveway with a rusty nail sticking out of it. My roommate stepped on it at four in the morning and had to go to the hospital. She missed her friend's funeral because she had to keep

Carolyn Zaikowski

her foot elevated for a week."

"That's terrible! This guy is something else, huh?"

"Yeah, man. He's a total character."

"Well, I gotta get going. I'll send you the notebooks," Sigmund Freud says, standing up. I'm positive he won't really. But the next day in the mail, four cardboard boxes filled with his notes are delivered right to my doorstep.

CASE STUDY #7: So I Go

She is constantly aware of the reality of death. This drives her to kiss everything she touches. She tries to kiss with her existence, which often manifests as fucking; sometimes she has to settle for kissing with her parts—lips, fingers, belongings, pens. She doesn't want to let anything go without saying goodbye, without wrapping up the box and throwing it down the river. I tell her how I feel; I try to live clearly. It's all I can do. The universe charges forward with or without me in it, whether or not we're in it together, whether or not we're standing on the edge looking over at the next thing. On the back porch, as I smoke a cigarette, I decide to imagine her walking up the steps. She's whispering: "Now drink the wine from the goblet and wait for the explosion to reach its blur. You will feel a sense of being airborne just before you reach the lichen." She hands me a letter and a pile of papers: Dear friend: Will you audition for the part of me? Here is the script. Memorize it well. Don't forget all of the steps to the dance during the second act. Don't have that dream again. Love you

Disappearing slowly, she dares me to be an artist. She says, if you agree to be an artist, I will show you the most wonderful thing that exists. But you can't know about it till you learn how to play this guitar upside-down. How to smash this safety glass. How to balance this easel on your toe. You can't be an artist

until you create the ugliest painting, poem, and song
in the world.

Behind her, near the fence, a man tries to hide while
he takes a drink; he doesn't taste it, but his teeth are
stained red. He imagines pushing her into the river.
She would be fine, he thinks to himself; the water
is moving quickly but it's only about knee-high. He
grabs and kisses her. The bottle of wine falls into the
river. They both feel guilty about littering, but they
know they will never see each other again, so they
let the bottle bob with the current to the poor part
of the city.

Now they're floating past the bottle. I can hardly
hear her now; she's just a gaseous wisp. "Darling,
you might miss your only opportunity to see the
lichen," she's calling to me. Her voice is hoarse. "If
this happens, write to me. I will send you a photograph or painting of the lichen. My address can
be found on the empty end of the ink tube in your
pen. But you really don't want to miss this chance!
To never see the lichen, I think, would qualify as a
travesty, or maybe a tragedy. So go now, before the
lichens start to recognize human faces; they might
respond by disappearing!"

So I go to the edge of the mountain, where I find a
straight cliff and a cloud that goes forever. I'm two
miles above sea level, surrounded by fossils. There's

no lichen. It doesn't matter; I've never met her—or have I?—either way, we share a face. She's the one who gave me all of space and time. The one who sculpted a photograph of god and let me see it. I remember the umbrella under which she sat, saintly.

I'm happy and calm in the cloud, but everyone else wants the view, says the cloud is the wrong thing. So I go. At a coffee shop in New Mexico, a little boy is dressed like a little girl and it makes everybody sad except me. He says, "The wall is too big for you. You deserve a flat surface, but this one is way over the top! It's a ridiculous expanse—it's overtaking existence. Run!" I tell him to shut up. Then, at the same coffee shop in New Mexico, I hear country music. A train passes by the coffee shop in New Mexico. No it doesn't; I'm imagining things. I've never met her, but that isn't true. In a strange land I spent several nights with her. I watched her run toward the lichen-less cliff and stop just in time to permeate it. On Monday, she will have been dead for three months.

She is happy. She is lethargic. She has a moustache. No, she doesn't have a moustache. What kind of ruins will she create? She is handfed. She is tired. She is not tired. She holds scraps of beaten mush. She holds papery little lambs. She throws them into a pile one by one and counts them. She stops at ten and wonders, is ten a lot or only a little bit of papery little lambs? She wants to know how many she will need in order to have a lot, but she is too awake to decide.

This is not the end of the story. Fields of white usually make me anxious. This one does not. Wait, this is wrong. I've gone to the coffee shop, I didn't remember. Here, away from the cloud, she holds scraps of beaten men as she watches the bikers. Is one of them the brother I have never met? You are, you there. I can tell by your gaunt face and by the way you carry your guitar; that's how our father carried his. I am so tired; it haunts me. You are so tired; it haunts me. We are all wronged sleepers. But she is paper. She cuts and writes on herself, so she is not lethargic. The brother who I have never met rides his motorcycle to the cliff I once visited. The bell rings. The light is green above the bell. The green rings. But before he goes, at a coffee shop in New Mexico, my brother asks me to write while he takes my picture.

CASE STUDY #8: Revolution

We can smash the state together if you would just
listen to me. If only you'd put my dick in your mouth,
there'd be a revolution. Don't worry, you're just feeling overemotional. It's that time of the month. You
need to lose weight. I only say that because I know
how self-conscious you are and I'm trying to help,
and besides, if you over-eat that means you are wast-
ing the earth's resources, and peak oil's coming. Trust
me, you should get an abortion. Don't you know how
many radicals fought for your right to abort my baby?
Look at that billboard. The man is holding a penis/
beer and the woman wants it, she's asking for it, do
you get it, it's like a beer but it's also like a dick. Put
down your notebook and penis-pen. Come to the
rally on the Boston Common with me. Everyone'll
see us. Give me a blowjob and be gentle. Why are
you being so gentle? Don't you want people to think
you're strong? If you would only just stick with me
maybe you'd figure it out, maybe I'd get off your case,
'cause I respect you, I love you, I'm not a sexist, I'm
not a racist, I'm not a sexist, I'm not a racist, I'm not
a sexist, I'm not a racist, and I'm not a sexist.

CASE STUDY #9: Box

Dream—in the burning house, I run to save a box
filled with your memories. You wave goodbye from
the window. When I wake up, I remember you're
dead. What the fuck? Oh, how she dreams of starving
like you starved, so softly; of having that propensity
for obsession, for total action. She pities and envies
your bones because, having seen you erased, it's the
only thing she understands. She wants to be a tiny
rainstorm, a sprinkle of a lunatic. She wants to be the
daintiest drink. She thinks you don't know. Dream—
the universe is pink, the same exact color of raspberry
sorbet, and I am locked in a bunker with all of the
chosen people, watching it implode from god's greatest movie screen. Dream—your face is missing a nose
and eyes. I give you mine.

Your tater tots are burning; better get out of yourself,
better turn the oven off. Your ice is melting in your
whiskey. Ground yourself. Ask: Where did you put
the box? What do you see in this moment? Oh, some
big fish. Lots of toys. Tiny broken trucks. Ticket
stubs. Jimi Hendrix records. Blue candles, unlit,
that want to smell like the ocean but only smell like
salty soap. Glass tables that you really don't want to
break; they're not yours. This isn't your house. You
have no house. You do not even have a body, yet you
are so clumsy.

Here's a true story: The last thing she ever said to you was, "I'd tell you that I love you, but I don't think you have the capacity to believe me." The last thing you ever said to her was, "I have never been anything but good to you. I didn't ask to be alive. I want to die. You should be ashamed of yourself." What this might mean is that you are an episode. You are mind.

The world's largest recycled object is a boat made out of Popsicle sticks, and it's in the Netherlands. This is what you heard on the news today. A duck walked into a corner store in London. That was on the news, too. These aren't dreams. I even looked them up on the internet to make sure.

Listen. God is trying to find me. If he comes, tell him I'm not here. Tell him I'm in the shower. Tell him I'm at the bar.

CASE STUDY #10: Shakespeare

They are sitting in their apartment eating salads and drinking Sambuca. She wants to touch his passionate eyes with her finger, so she does. "This is historic," she says as she feels the tip of her index finger on her right hand meeting the bulbous flesh of his left eye. Here is the problem: The moment the two surfaces make contact, her psyche becomes overrun with the desire to push. So she pushes her finger into his eye, and she pushes further, and she pushes further still. Because he hates himself, he doesn't scream.

She pushes her finger into his eye until a little pop can be heard and a spurt of blood arrives in the air between them, at which time she gasps, vomits, and runs from the room. They never see each other again, but he can never quite see properly after that day anyways.

It is complete; he is beautiful now. He thanks her silently.

Once outside, she wipes her hand on her jeans and notices that the light inside her is getting dimmer. She thinks about the constant stress that molecules are under and how ugly her atoms must be. From some background, perhaps from behind the apartment building, the ghost of an opera singer—a mezzo soprano—is singing Gladys Knight's "Midnight Train to Georgia".

She tries to find the ghost. She is panicked with her need to find the ghost. She runs behind the apartment building; she can still hear the song. She hits her ears with her fists. She picks up a rock that is about the size of her palm and throws it; her arm is the saddest lever. It hits the side of the brick apartment building, letting off a "ping" that seems too high in volume and too strange in tone, but it makes the singing stop.

OPERA: The telling of a story through music, generally on a stage. MUSICAL: A play in which songs are used for some of the story, but most of the story is presented through speech. SHAKESPEARE: Guy who wrote a bunch of stuff in England a long time ago. SHAKESPEARE: Borachio. Number one master of hiding things in text. The poison of that lies in you to temper go you to the prince your brother SHAKESPEARE: Gay pervert. SHAKESPEARE: Perhaps not as well known in his time as the guy who wrote the story about the guy who sold his soul to the devil.

"What is the cut on your leg from?"

"Is this the live version?"

"What the fuck is going on?"

SHAKESPEARE: A revolutionary who carried a pen as large as a continent in his soul's hand.

"Is this you, in this picture? Did you really used to have dreadlocks? Why don't you have that dimple anymore? I didn't know dimples could go away? Do your question marks look like the letter S or the number 7?" Nobody has eyes anymore.

SHAKESPEARE: A man, born in Stratford-upon-Avon, who knew not what he loved.

"I wish I could be more like you. The way you hold yourself as if there is a wooden board in your spine. You are so stoic and you aren't even a soldier. Come here, love. Come here."

SHAKESPEARE: Tomorrow and tomorrow and tomorrow creeps in this petty pace from day to day till the last syllable of recorded time and all our yesterdays have lighted fools the way to dusty death out out brief candle life is but

"Grandma, I wish I could've been more like you"

SHAKESPEARE: Famous person who might have collaborated and/or had ghost writers.

"Mom, I wish I could've been more like you"

SHAKESPEARE: Man whose question marks looked neither like the letter S or the number 7.

"Aunty, I wish I could've been more like you"

SHAKESPEARE: Maker of love in regards to iambic pentameter.

She is not a grandmother, stepmother, or mother. She is a daughter, sister, niece, aunt, stepdaughter, and granddaughter. She is not a son, stepfather, or father. She is not a brother or a grandson. She is not a nephew, uncle, stepson, or grandfather. Her dead aunt called her today and said, Trust me. So she said, I do. She said SHAKESPEARE IS A MAN WHO ATTEMPTED TO FILL IN THE BLANK YOU WILL ALWAYS HAVE.

CASE STUDY #11: Orwell

There is nothing more heartbreaking than somebody refusing to believe that you love them. At least, this is my experience. Then again, I have never been in a war; I imagine that would be the most heartbreaking thing in the world. In any case, with you, I must continually prepare myself for this refusal. It's okay; I know you're not reading this. Let me just say I used to think you were crazy because you were so smart, like a mad scientist. Now I know better, which means I'm getting old.

So:

Dear George Orwell: When I was fifteen I went to London and saw the house of your birth. It has a little blue oval plaque on it that says *George Orwell Birthplace*. Across the street there was a man sitting on a bucket wrapped from head to toe in toilet paper, blowing bubbles at a wall. It was Valentine's Day and, back home, I was dating a rapist, but he didn't know he was a rapist and neither did I. My mom wouldn't let me call him because it was too expensive, not because he was a rapist. I had really bad acne. I'm pretty sure the only time I smiled in London was when I saw your house and oh, also, at the little inn where the room was haunted and the shower turned on by itself in the middle of the night. I smiled then, too. So drink it, Orwell; I'll give you my glass. A poet wrote "the woods are lovely, dark and deep, but I have promises to keep" etc. etc. I'm sure you knew that already. Will you sing it? Tell me what your favorite part of speech is. None of this is my fault. You asked me to be written. Are you over? How do I spell you? Do you have silent letters? What secrets do you put in your paintings? If you tell me, I promise to never let anybody know. Please, tell me, what does an island look like; did you grow up on one? Are you claustrophobic from it? Does your island have a golden plaque that says *My Island Only?* Do you know what the difference is between stretching and breaking? Because I don't. I have no formula. I need you; I don't know where I am or where I've been. I've lost the planet, but you're an entire alphabet made of birch trees and mountains. And what will I do if the last page is ripped? Do I coddle it? Do I cry? Do I celebrate? There is nothing I can do. I have thrown you the sloppy ball and you are looking at it. Love you.

CASE STUDY #12: South Station, Boston

At South Station in Boston, there is a tiny lady with gray hair and a limp. She doesn't speak English. She's trying to sell candies from her hand. She approaches two cops and holds the candies out to them. "We already told you once," the first cop warns in his thick New England accent. She doesn't understand his language, so she holds the candies out again. "We'll put you in jail," says the second cop. "Jail," parrots the first, as he waves his handcuffs at her. She walks outside, in the direction of Chinatown. Shakespeare, oh Shakespeare, do you see?

The young woman near the other door, she stands alone with an invisible thing. She can feel it melt into her hands, her stomach, her genitals; eventually it becomes knives in her blood. It doesn't just seep into her eyes, it actually becomes her eyes. She feels her corneas shifting, her lenses accommodating, her retinas stretching. It harnesses all her power into itself until she is nothing but a circular railroad track upon which it will ride forever if not derailed by something significantly larger. She can feel herself being overridden. She knows what is happening, but she can't seem to stop it; this fact tortures her. So she performs experiments that are specifically designed to keep her mind alert. She does crossword puzzles. She makes things out of clay, presses her thumbs into the tiny gray bubbles. She writes new

languages on paper with a pen, sometimes with a
fat marker, but she never shows them to anybody.
She definitely doesn't show them to any cops. This
way, she has control over a secret. She seals and
opens envelopes, closes and shuts doors. She walks
through the Chinatown streets as slowly as she can
while counting anthills and beauty parlors. But
mostly, she knit scarves. The scarves she makes are
not pretty, at least she doesn't think so; they're filled
with all kinds of holes. She uses the cheapest yarn
she can find. She makes them in the middle of the
summer if she has to, when nobody wants to touch
yarn because of how sweat feels against it. She has a
large pile of scarves under her bed and tries to give
them away to everyone she meets.

How many places were you in when the bridge
collapsed? She was in several. I was in any number of
places between one and forty-seven. She was walking around; I was stationary. It was not a footbridge.
It had cars on it. What could possibly have made it
fall? The Mississippi River, I imagine, is very large
and cold. But I've never seen it, let alone touched it.
Now all the cars are in it. They say, "They don't think
the bus went into the water but they do think some
children were injured."

She's sinking to the bottom. Open your window;
don't wait until the glass shatters. Develop gills. Give
me permission to dive into and over the beyond to

see her off. I will eat the algae. I will go to the crabs. I will touch her nose with mine, I will touch her ear one more time before she becomes sand on that river-bank, before she becomes fish food or a god's eye.

"Some survivors are being carried up the riverbank"

Under the bridge, she once held a list:

Things I See In Santa Fe, New Mexico, United States of America:

> Water Street public parking lot
> Bobby's Cosmetics
> El Centra
> Sun Country Traders
> Cold Stone Creamery
> Five & Dime
> Chile Shop
> Subway
> Feathers of Heaven
> Guadalupano Imports

IX.
FINAL ASSESSMENT

ANNOUNCEMENT

FINAL ASSESSMENT

What is the age, color, and precipice-place of your inner child, and do you cry for her at night? Pick one:

A. She is a beautiful end, doing ballet through a dream, up and down the hallway with the floating walls. Pointing our toes towards her, we think about whether or not it is wise to touch her shadow, which is laser-like and can sear locks. Even though her tutu looks like a drawing of a tutu, we know it is her, for sure, dancing ridiculously, that huge mouth of teeth; she's trotting around and under and through, her huge mouth inhibited by stones. Automobiles roar out of the place where she teeters, loving a cliff, wings bouncing against her from all sides.

B. One time a telephone cord, delighting all of the bugs, visited my home. You, in it, said there was a thing or two that was wonderful about being gone. I, a white cloth, cackled. You knew I never really believed in your ability to end.

C. A jail knocks on the first window it sees and wants to know if there is a room available. The foreman says Scram, Jail, this is an important project we're trying to complete, and you take up too much space. The jail takes a step backwards and grabs the first child it sees and puts the child in itself. Ha! They may never understand me, but at least I have their child in myself, so they will always need me, he thinks.

A_   **B_**

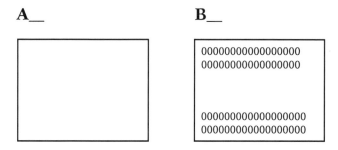

Which of the above boxes do you enjoy more? Please place an X above your selected box. You may only choose one box. This test will be used to determine your level of raw yet hearty connection to the mythology and ruling archetypes of your sliver of the collective unconscious as described by Carl Gustav Jung in the pre- and post- World War Two years may he rest in peace lord almighty in the Judeo-Christian heaven or one of the other heavens and also in the cosmos beyond our mortal understanding in head, heart, hand, and gut.

Please use the below space to create your representation of the existential blur:

How, when, where, and why do you store your intensity?

Are you an accurate representation of yourself? Explain your answer using stories.

Have you or will you ever decide to fearlessly love a stranger?

Have you ever written about your overwhelming desire to drink the wine that is eternity's blood? Why or why not?

Will you speak freely of your oldest dream?

How many solutions do you have?

What is the shape of your invisible bottle of white ink?

ATTENTION

The bulldozer is heading toward the lichens. Please gather all of your loved ones and form a circle around the lichens with your bodies. Do not return to your daily life until you have made sure that the bulldozer is gone forever.

Thank you.

X.
FINAL ANALYSES

Pull Your Skin Back With Tape

Fuck Maps

**In a Dream, I Dance by Myself,
and I Collapse**

PULL YOUR SKIN BACK WITH TAPE

I.

I need your help. I need it for free. I am so sorry that I can't pay you, but there isn't much time left, and I need to know: For what did you pray when you were sitting on the mountain? I am not sure what material my heart is made out of or what shape it is, if it has sticks in its rivers, if its reflections are blocked by trees. If so, did I plant those trees on purpose or did they grow on their own? Do they make shadows in the night? Was I with you on the mountain or was I far below? Please help me. I've exposed almost everything.

II.

Nobody knows much about her. She dresses up like a man and hops trains; that's how she got here. She does odd jobs like painting, gardening, lawn-mowing, cigarette-rolling, and knitting in exchange for a room in a hidden house. She doesn't own a bed. The only thing she has is a snare drum that she found in a field, next to an old car part. She takes off the top of the snare drum, hides her pens and paper inside, puts her ear up next to it, and listens. She must do this at least once in order to get to sleep at night.

She never knew her parents, though she's pretty
sure they're still alive somewhere in Washington or
California. She can't figure out whether or not she is
an orphan.

The hidden house is crooked. She fills a bookshelf
and stabilizes it with the Book of Mormon under one
corner and a pile of feminist zines under the other.
The house is black, with one pink shingle on the
porch which she denies having painted. In the living
room lies a snare drum that nobody ever touches.

She thinks to herself, oh god, people really do hang
out at the mall. She steals rolls of toilet paper from
coffee shop bathrooms. She watches trashy daytime
television shows and is not embarrassed about it. She
notes that in the food court at the mall, the flowers
are in full bloom; she sees that there is mascara everywhere, on eyes, in stores. She is a quasi-Buddha. Rub
her stomach or her head for good luck.

She imagines holding you in your most vulnerable
moment. This way, you will love her.

III.
She scares me. She's always competing for diseases.
She has love bursting out of her and she isn't always
in control of what she does with it. When I remember
my dreams of her, I try to convince myself she's just

a symbol. She doesn't take me seriously when I tell her, in my mind, with my loudest thoughts, to forget me; when I tell her that we shouldn't matter to one another. She drinks too much; she is in pain. I love in her in my sleep and, once awake, I try to breathe her away. Yet I can't shake her. Can't erase her from the space of my space. After all this time I still feel her hand on my back. I still see her under the tree, near the bottom of the mountain. I try to pretend she's not there; I experiment with anti-visions. I close my eyes briefly and she fades into the blur; she is green, then clear, but still she remains in all valleys.

I test my will to hold myself in. She is already ghost, but she doesn't know it yet. Her body is still alive. She would look beautiful as a corpse. In my mind, I cut the sin out of her. I kill her unborn baby. I run her off the road in a dream. I have written a book about her. In the end of it, she dies.

It's getting late. God is looking for her mightily. She says, "If I never played music or performed again, I would be sad. If I never wrote again, I would die. Do you understand?"

IV.
Caught in the wheel of you, I must not filter. I must go through. I saw you on the bus two months after it happened. When we made eye contact, I ran off at

the next stop. I decided it must have been an accident that you were near me, a chance encounter.

Once home, I turned on the TV. It said buy and sell everything, eat everything from eyeball to eyeball, from tongue to tooth, I want to buy new hands, I will disappear for you if I must, erasure is a gift buy buy sell sell. It said you are food, you are meat, you eat and are objects. You obsess over your baby's belly. Anything for baby. Gerber Gerber Gerber Gerber. Zoloft Zoloft Zoloft Zoloft. Pull your skin back with tape.

The white glow goes into me. And you there, you, important entity, and you, useful function, how are you? You are the ladder I climb. You are a rope and a destination, you are the embryo, the RNA, the DNA, all of the amino acids.

V.

Neither of us answers the door or the phone. It might be a military recruiter, a Jehovah's Witness. It might be one of our fathers.

I sip from her dissociation like a martini through a straw. She has no idea where she will end up if she climbs me. She doesn't know how strong or weak my ability to forget about her is.

Weeks later, she thought she saw me, but it was really just a person with my haircut; no, just my hair color. Her memory of me likes to lie and play. She doesn't want to go. She bites me and I am infected, but she is not a snake or spider. I do not understand her, but I know she is the tree I loved, where my rope swing hung, until my parents cut it down when I was eleven. She stands at my window for a fraction of eternity. She asks me if I will go to her funeral if she dies, and I say yes without thinking. I know she will be always watching me from the secret swimming place. Like two backwards-facing magnets, we move because of each other, but in the wrong direction. She makes a cliff of herself and dares me to lean forward, further, further; nobody knows how long to hang on to the end of her.

VI.

This time, everything begins on a plane in Ohio, next to thunder, and moves downwards. Things begin when you are still within breathing distance of the plane. Things begin with dinosaurs and their eggs. With mounds of pillows. Explosions that're large and creative. Your finger poking my soul. A thousand-year old child. Catnip-laced drops of vanilla. The thing we call a wing that's so stupid and flat compared to a bird's. This time, everything begins in the hardware store I saw you at, right after I stole the orange and black notebooks. Your skin was there. There was molten and magma. This is not a dream.

Breathe. Breathe. It's just a toy gun. It's just a firework.

This begins. He is drunk, but he makes you get in the car. He's bigger than you. It's cold and you have no shoes. He starts driving even though you plead for him to pull over. Finally he does, near the field, behind the airport, off the main road. You jump out of the car. It's raining; no, it's more like November sleet. "I'm never giving you another ride again!" he bellows. You remember how you used to go to the airport to watch planes take off. Stoned, you would sit by the ocean, dangling your feet towards the harbor. The blue lights were always in a line. The red lights moved. For now, you walk without shoes to the 24-hour falafel restaurant near the hanger. You remember how the car had still been moving when you jumped out. It wasn't glamorous like in some action movie; he was only going about five miles an hour, probably less. No, you think to yourself; the car couldn't really have been moving.

This begins. Breathe. You are a train—chug on. You are an anchor—release. Your voice was the tree in my yard. Your voice is a sky that meets a ground after years spent longing for an ocean—it is a compromise, the decision to land.

This begins. You cry looking over the bridge, into the river that separates two cities; you think about how

your hair is finally long. You could jump, but you do
not want to be a mermaid or a fish.

VII.

"How is your mother? I heard she broke her arm and
has a metal plate in it now. What color is the metal
plate? What type of metal? Is it an alloy? Oh my god,
did you hear that Pluto isn't a planet anymore?" The
first boy plays his guitar on the broken couch. He
says he is homeless now. This means he is a couch-
crasher who will go back to his parents' house when
he runs out of the money they've given him. I am
bored of him; I always have been. He only plays
upstrokes. He won't play "Rocky Raccoon"; he
thinks The Beatles are for hippies. Lethargic, I eat a
pasty hummus wrap in the bowl-shaped chair that
smells of cat urine. In code, he brags about various
addictions. He makes tea with drugs in it, then makes
things hot on my favorite spoon and injects them into
his ankle veins with fake fervor.

The next boy comes. He picks up the guitar, starts to
play the arpeggios of The Beatles' "Because". I ask
him, "Doesn't my beauty distract you anymore?" He
replies, "It doesn't matter what I say. Nothing I say
or do will make you believe me." I dream of the food
I haven't eaten in days or years. I dream of so many
sauces. My eyes open slightly, my glasses foggy, my
pen foggy. It occurs to me that the trees outside the

window may have you, as god, waiting in them. I
hear the phone ringing from beneath some blanket
pile; I don't reach for it, but I hope it's you; I hope it's
all my lovers calling at once. All my lovers, they're
in an unspeakable abyss. I float above them, looking and lost, lost and honest, overwhelmed with the
sense of never being able to touch any of them again.

He puts down the guitar. "You should get some
lemon and put it in your tea. It will make your stomach feel better. I'm not worth getting sick over. Please,
let me make you some plain pasta. It will absorb your
stomach acid. Don't listen to the train squealing, it'll
only make you think about how you aren't on it. How
you are here, in this place with the bodies hanging off
the bridges, with the cars in the fields with the stuffed
up mufflers, with the fractured skulls and the failed
kidneys and everybody who wants to fight in a war."
The first boy returns, puts down my favorite spoon,
tells me he has learned so much about me from my
bookshelf. I tell him, "I do not owe it to you to be
nice, or brave."

VIII.

Here's the truth: There are several things you could
do right now. You could crack your knees; you
could open and close a door numerous times; you
could take a trip to the theater, or to the place where
air conditioners are made. You could steam some

broccoli. You could invest in a timeshare in Aspen, and you could ski there periodically, but that might be cold and costly, and you are not inclined towards wealth or ice. You could engage in mature dialogue with one of your lover's other lovers, who's sitting in a rocking chair on the other side of the room. You could torture yourself by imagining everything you know to be false. By planning unnecessary funerals. You could tell your best friend that her existence and her guitar playing have saved you. You could ask yourself: what temperature do you want your body/being to be at? And then admit sadly that you have no idea.

A young woman yells from the kitchen, "Remember that scene from *Ghost* with Patrick Swayze and Demi Moore, with the clay pots, and that song from the sixties? That was such a classic scene! Whatever needs to be done, I'll be around. I'm going to vacuum the floor now. I'm going to clean the dishes and wipe the circles out of the sink."

The empty rocking chair inhabits a cave, but in the darkness you float above the rocking chair, content. You hear the tears of a third boy but are not scared. No, you imagine them. This one you wanted so desperately to exist outside your window, he's all the way on the other side of the phone that doesn't ring. What button can he press to make you happy? You want to be what he cries. You don't know what crying means. It doesn't matter. Something that no one knows is keeping us safe and alive. You imagine hanging up the phone.

At some point, the second boy comes and comes. It is now, during this moment of orgasm, that you are both creator and created, ruining and being ruined; the ultimate implosion and explosion of life-force. It is now that you see everything at once. How did it not occur to anyone that maybe the opposite of death isn't life, maybe it is sex? Maybe sex and life are the same phenomenon. At the very least, they are both explosions. How did it not occur to anyone that perhaps the big bang was the first orgasm.

XI.

Now I am fucking you and I am thinking, of course, this is the answer. This is everything I've been trying to see. I picture all kinds of people floating by on an unraveling film reel, you and you and you and in this moment we are all together, accounted for, safe; even you who are far away, I feel you. You who are dead who I loved back then; you are here, too. I touch your faces. I don't even want you back anymore, you who I kissed in the living room of my father's house, you with your tiny eyes; for so long, I had forgotten what you looked like and I couldn't find your picture. And you who makes me want to tear my face off, you're here too, and I love you. I want to let you all know that everything will be okay. The paper is being burned, the grass is growing and dying with all of us in it. The earth-orgasm happens and then we're done and you say to me, "This is life. This is death. This is god. This is a flower in a garden. This is a garbage can. This is the hall we walk down every morning. This is marriage, a house, and children. This is us fighting and making up. This is our college degree. In this moment, everything has already happened at once. It doesn't matter if we never see each other again. Because of this moment we have already had an entire life together." Stay with and in me. It is not your body that is holding my body, or mine that is holding yours. It is just the universe lying in a bed, breathing, creating weather and trees underneath weather.

Carolyn Zaikowski

FUCK MAPS

What if I return to the open space, only to find that the body writes itself, pen on finger, bomb in hand? The universe doesn't make any sense. Sometimes I find that beautiful and sometimes I find it horrible, but either way it owns me. The texture of light, the holes poked in space, paper being burned. Cells relate and embrace. Cells remember a time when they had each other but were separated by some mannish thought-bolt. The indefinable blur is where everything everythings. Right in that eye, we used to be together in our fear instead of hurting one another because of it. The potential that wants. The threshold where revolution bakes bread. Love-junk. Muscle folds. The blood-brain barrier. The blur of my body writes me into existence and you out of it.

Why does the word "sausage" appear to me? Why "cracked wheat?" Some things:

> –The flavor of your kidneys. The time you took me aside at the famous diplomat's wedding to show me a crack in the wall within which, you thought, lived all types of potential gods.

> –Roller-skating with you over other people's lawns and trampling geraniums with our wheels. It was the 1950s.

–The color of the tie you wore that time, and how you hated ties.

–I threw my hair over the balcony and you climbed into the window on my braid. It was midnight. I didn't know whether or not you were a monster, but I didn't mind monsters.

–The toaster oven exploding with wet oil, at least that's what I think I remember.

Hurry up and think with me: There is no god, or maybe there is. You are dead and heaven is shaped like a small cave near an ocean at the Tropic of Capricorn. The universe is a novel and a poem and a painting. Smoke doesn't really exist, because you can put your hand through it. I hate the things I love and need. If you watch paper burn, you can understand the nature of nature. Pain persists without elegance but it doesn't reign. Life has the potential to be a lullaby. In some significant but foggy way, you will own me forever. The seventh dimension makes no sense. Fuck maps. Where I am headed is not on a map. Where you are is outer. You can't just go around trying to map everything. Some dimensions simply defy maps and re-create them. As for here, you will never be able to get here; all's gone. My map moves behind me and will never catch up. Its inherent lag causes it to outdate itself immediately. What map do you use in death? Right. Fuck maps. Concepts continually dissipate and some of them straight up explode. Eternity's blood smells like a basement and pours itself out in the shape of a too-long tie. So I don't store, but I don't burn, either. That's all.

–I am very interested in other people's medications. If I see a bottle that isn't mine I look up the name of the medication and somehow it seems I know that person better even if all they have for an ailment is hay fever. Another secret is that I steal old photographs from trash piles. Especially after people move. I stake out moving couples in my neighborhood and watch them throw their trash away. If a tree falls in the woods, and there's no one around to hear it, and it's a secret, does it matter if you tell people how much electricity the tree might have conducted when it hit the ground?

–Here is a fable: I throw my hair over the balcony and you climb into the window via my braid at midnight. I do not know whether or not you are a monster. I do not mind monsters. I find the rectangle screws at your temple vaguely attractive and your metal heart is such a charming sphere. Here is a fable: you are the magical lady of the future. Here is a fable mixed with a theory: I have joy. I hold it; sometimes that's a secret. Or is it a fable. Or a monster.

IN A DREAM, I DANCE BY MYSELF, AND I COLLAPSE

Dream—at a nursing home, an elderly man with Alzheimer's walks out the metal door, onto an empty patio made of concrete. He says into a stark nothing-ness, *"Am I here? Am I even here?"* I force myself, or maybe the elderly man forces me, to wake up. I am staring at the wall in the room I've never slept in before and the elderly man is in my throat, knocking on my esophagus, which is now the dream-door. I turn over. There is a person next to me with whom I have never slept in the same bed, who told me yesterday that he looked at his hands and, for the first time, saw a man's hands instead of a boy's. I remember all those times looking at my own hand and seeing a small imposter of my father's. Those broken nails and ticks of my wrist. Those finger-taps on steering wheels.

Dream—a five floor house, an attic filled with unpacked luggage; I find the girl with the two-toned hair but who I am really looking for is my boyfriend. I wake up again to the person with whom I have never slept in the same bed. I wonder if I feel guilty. A sense of homeless joy and sadness is in me. He makes me quinoa with almond milk and cinnamon and I think about cats and how death must be really painless.

Dream—I check myself into the hospital and the doctor berates me in front of all of the tall students in white coats. I remember screaming at him, I remember how I tell him that this is real life and not a television show, and he says well then let your heart erode and I tell him he is an asshole and he tells me I have not yet proven that I care about being alive. There are floating fractals everywhere, they're far beyond coffee, beyond cannibalism, beyond the possibility of eating myself. I run down the hall frantic and I still have a pulse and I can't remember which part of this is a dream.

Dream—the person whose name I will not say comes to me asks me if my mother's memories are real. I tell him I don't know my mouth is gone for you.

Dream—I don't remember when you did what I won't say, I don't remember when you pushed me against the wet paint or how I could see that your eyes didn't want to be a weapon; I don't remember the name you called me; I don't remember how you broke my secret place, destroyed my books and my bed. Dream—you are the cracks around whom I try to build a wall. Dream—I don't remember your barrels filled with beer cans or how you smelled of alcohol's sweat in the morning or how I watched The Muppets with the green blanket on my lap; I don't remember your running sneakers or the exercise videos; I don't remember in the 80s when running was a fad and Jane

Fonda was an anorexic guru in neon instead of a radical antiwar protester in Vietnam; I don't remember vomiting on the countertop when I broke your favorite mug, which fell out of the freezer; I don't remember that terrible thing you said when I was eating soggy cereal on the wooden bench or how I loved to use the enormous serving spoon to eat cereal. Dream—I make up a crime and I try to convince people

I don't remember how you smashed the plate; that tile, those stairs

The two of you laughing in the living room degrading women together; how I told you about my biggest secret and you turned towards an open window; I don't remember the face you made when you were disappointed

Dream—I don't remember when the police came or how I lied; the homeless man who slept on the floor; the toy airplane you smashed on the basketball court; the way you left me, the way you left an orphan, and the way you left a whore. Dream—I am not afraid

Dream—You and your Mohawk. Your dog. You run. You drink a dainty drink. You watch the Yankees vs. some team no one cares about. You wonder why all baseball announcers sound the same. You think about Jamaica. You feel guilty for your paleness— you feel stupid—you don't even know how to spell

Carolyn Zaikowski

"stupid". Suddenly you want to hide your dreadlocks.
I feel guilty for missing you and I will never tell you.
The man in jeans and a Hawaiian shirt looks at a
bottle of Tabasco sauce. I am alone in a Mexican
restaurant. I wonder if I'll get old. I whisper under a
green blanket, Where are you? I miss you so much
I would risk being dead if it meant seeing you one
more time. I want you to tell me what death means
and how you feel now, I want you to tell me if you
are happy, if you are safe, if you finally love yourself,
I want to know if you are drinking whiskey, if you
are warm, if you have blankets. I want to know if
you will be waiting for me when I die so I don't have
to be a lonely reflection on a vast undiscovered sea;
sometimes I swear to god I can feel you even though
I know you don't exist anymore. I know because
I saw your body without you in it, I touched your
chest, and I spoke to you as you lay in quietly in your
casket, and this is all the proof I'm supposed to need

I wrote this for you: Once there was a pen who
wanted to learn how to write. When no one was
looking, she practiced and practiced and practiced.
This went on for years until she became the most
wonderful calligrapher in all the universe and she
even wrote her own set of codes which might have
been a language. The only problem was that no one
knew the pen had taught herself how to write so
nobody knew that she had become the most wonderful calligrapher in all the universe and definitely

nobody knew about her set of codes that were maybe a language. And so she lived in the dark solitude of her inkwell for all eternity with this secret.

Dear Sir, it is very strange to know I could never see you again. I suppose this is a true thing for all people, at all times; anyone could die or disappear at any juncture, become an infinite fractal; I suppose it is true that you and I might represent everything: A quick fucked up wonderful ride in a strange land that makes no sense and then is over. Thank you for accompanying me. Love you

Dream—on the cliff near the ocean I ask you if you are safe, if you are calm; you disappear

Dream—"Dennis, what's up buddy? It seems the technical requirements are breaking down access to the wide life stream. Must be in another document."

Do you hear the guitar?

"Got it, got it. So what we're gonna do is we're gonna go in there and submit the software under section six."

Do you hear the guitar?

"What's up, Gus. I just got off the phone with Dennis. What we're gonna do is we're gonna go in on top of that and submit to section six."

You walk away to fill up your cornstarch cup with filtered water, but I want to know the rest of what you are going to tell Gus. Are you going to lie about what Dennis said? Are you going to tell the story about section six correctly?

"You. You."

And the wide life stream?

Dream—here's a dream—peace, no pain. I dreamt that in a meat locker you raped me and it was freezing. I dreamt that in the pile of leaves in the park in Roxbury you raped me and I had no flashlight and it was freezing. I dreamt that in the back of the hidden hospital you jumped out of a trash can became the largest person in the world and raped me and it was freezing. A dream—everyone loves things so nothing hurts. Here's a dream—you live. I know because I see you in the Chinese animal sanctuary that I assume represents peace and there is a purple bear and there are trees who say, "Everything is safe now, you are with me." Dream—you never stop telling your story. Dream—I trust the mess. Dream—I am worried about swimming across a lake in Bihar that keeps changing shape and depth. Dream—the island in the middle of the tsunami is mine and it is untouched. Dream—I rush to save seagulls and kittens from an exploding ocean. Here's a dream— everything is permitted. I fuck you, which will never happen in waking life. But in a dream I don't worry about touching you, ruining you in that way. In a dream, I dance by myself, and I collapse.

OFFICIAL

CCM ⚫

GET OUT OF JAIL
* VOUCHER *

- -

Tear this out.

Skip that social event.

It's okay.

You don't have to go if you don't want to. Pick up
the book you just bought. Open to the first page.
You'll thank us by the third paragraph.

If friends ask why you were a no-show, show them
this voucher.

You'll be fine.

- -

We're coping.

⚫